Jessica Moran is a licensed marriage and family therapist living in San Diego, California. She specializes in helping children overcome their anxieties, fears, and maladaptive behaviors to live their fullest and happiest life. When she is not working with children, she enjoys spending time with her husband, daughter, and two dogs.

ALLIE THE ALLIGATOR GETS
ANXIOUS

JESSICA MORAN

Austin Macauley Publishers™
LONDON · CAMBRIDGE · NEW YORK · SHARJAH

ISBN 9781528985758 (Paperback)
ISBN 9781528985765 (ePub-e-book)

www.austinmacauley.com

First Published (2021)
Austin Macauley Publishers Ltd
25 Canada Square
Canary Wharf
London
E14 5LQ

Allie is an alligator.
Allie likes to ride bikes, go to the park,
and paint.
Allie has a best friend named Emma.

Emma loves to try new things, like surfing, eating new foods, and sleepovers.

But trying new things makes
Allie feel funny.
Emma invites Allie to go to the water park
to ride the giant slides.
This makes Allie feel funny.

Allie tells her mother that she feels funny
and does not want to go to the water park.

Allie's mother asks,
"Do you have butterflies in your
tummy?"
Allie is confused.

Allie's mother explains, "Sometimes when we try new things, we get a funny feeling in our tummy. As if butterflies were fluttering around in our tummies. That funny feeling is called anxiety."

Allie whispers, "Does it always feel like butterflies?"

Allie's mother giggles, "No, sometimes it will feel like butterflies, sometimes it will feel like we can't sit still, as if our chest has something heavy on top of it, or we cannot catch our breath."

Allie cries, "What can I do?"

Allies mother states, "It is okay to feel anxious.
But there are many things that we can do
to feel better.
You can try to count to ten,
take 5 deep breaths, or listen to music."

Allie practices taking deep breaths every day
when she thinks about the big water slide.
Each time she practices,
she feels a little less anxious.

Finally, when the day comes for Allie to go to the water park with Emma, Allie no longer feels anxious.

Allie tries a small water slide first,
practicing her deep breathing.
Then she was ready for the big water slide.

Allie takes a few deep breaths and
walks up to the big water slide.

Emma encourages her,
"You can do it Allie! It will be fun!"

Allie takes one more deep
breath and goes down the big
water slide.

"Wheee!!! Yippee! Whoa!"
Allie cries as
she zooms down the big water slide.

Allie loved the big water slide!

And thinks, "I can work
though my anxiety to find new
things that I enjoy!"

Therapeutic Companion to Allie the Alligator Gets Anxious: What makes you Anxious

a. Goal: Have child identify times in their life that they feel anxiety.

b. Activity: Drawing Activity.

c. Instructions: Explain your child "Everyone feels anxious sometimes and that is okay. Draw or write about a time that made you feel anxious." After the child has completed the drawing talk to them about what they have drawn. Use the coping skills from the story (counting, deep breathing, or listing to music) to help your child through the anxious feelings.

d. Materials: Paper and drawing materials, such as crayons or markers.

How to be calm

a. Goal: Have child experience what it is like to be calm

b. Activity: Coloring Activity.

c. Instructions: Explain your child, "We have talked about what it feels like to be anxious. But now let's feel what it is like to be calm. Take some time to color this picture of Allie from the story we read and focus on being relaxed while you color."

d. Materials: Allie the Alligator coloring page and drawing materials, such as crayons or markers.

Breaking Down Anxiety Walls

a. Goal: Create an anxiety hierarchy to allow for more the in-depth areas of anxiety.

b. Activity:

i. Begins by explaining, "feelings of anxiety act like walls that keep us from trying new things or doing things that we might enjoy."

ii. Give child blocks, and tells them while modeling, "sometimes a feeling of anxiety is small and it only builds a small wall." Put two blocks together. "But sometimes our feelings of anxiety are big and make a great big wall." Model a larger wall by putting multiple blocks together.

iii. Continue by allowing the child to create his or her own walls, "Can you think of the times where you felt anxious and make a wall for each situation."

iv. Allow the child the time to think and create his or her own set of walls.

v. When the child has completed creating the walls, ask the child to state, without explaining, what each wall represents. Make sure to label each of the walls.

vi. The child is then asked to put each anxiety listed in order from most anxiety provoking to least anxiety provoking.

vii. Assist the child in creating a code word to use when discussing anxieties.

1. Explain, "Sometimes even talking about the things that make us anxious can make us feel overwhelmed. If you ever feel overwhelmed while we are talking about anxiety, say the codeword and we will immediately stop the conversation and cool down."

viii. Therapist or parent will then deeply process each wall or anxiety that the child has identified, starting with the least anxiety provoking to the most anxiety provoking. This will take several therapeutic sessions or days.

c. Blocks

Alligator Mandala

a. Goal: Increase mindfulness and reduce feelings of anxiety by shifting the child's focus. Therapist or parent to introduce mindfulness techniques at an age appropriate level.

b. Activity: Color the mandala

c. Materials: Allie the Alligator's Mother Mandala and drawing materials, such as crayons or markers.

CPSIA information can be obtained
at www.ICGtesting.com
Printed in the USA
LVHW070706190121
676860LV00005B/209